Legs, No Legs

Written by Mary Jones

Some animals have legs,
and some animals
have no legs.
Some animals can
grow new legs!

3

This insect has
a lot of legs.
It has little claws
on its legs.
The claws can help
the insect walk.

centipede

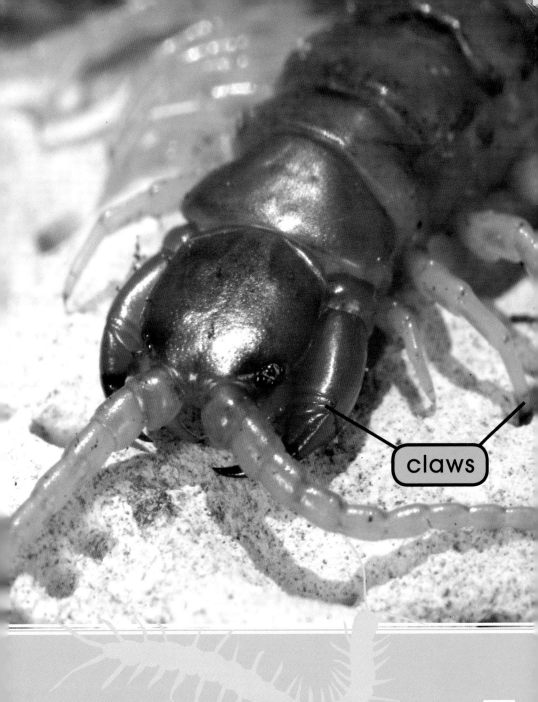

claws

This spider has eight legs.
Spiders can go fast
on their eight legs.
When a leg comes off,
the spider grows
a new leg.

This crab has eight legs.
Its legs are for walking.
It can get food
with its legs, too.
When a leg comes off,
the crab grows
a new leg.

crab

This starfish has five legs.
When a leg comes off,
the starfish grows
a new leg.

new legs

starfish

This snake has no legs,
but it goes fast.
It can go in and out
of the grass.

snake

This snail has no legs,
but it can't go fast.

snail

Animals with Legs

A lot of legs

8 legs

5 legs

Animals with No Legs

Index

animals with legs:

animals with no legs:

Guide Notes

Title: Legs, No Legs
Stage: Early (3) – Blue

Genre: Nonfiction
Approach: Guided Reading
Processes: Thinking Critically, Exploring Language, Processing Information
Written and Visual Focus: Photographs (static images), Index, Labels, Caption
Word Count: 131

THINKING CRITICALLY
(sample questions)
- Look at the front cover and the title. Ask the children what they know about animals with legs and animals without legs.
- Look at the title and read it to the children.
- Focus the children's attention on the index. Ask: "What are you going to find out about in this book?"
- If you want to find out about a centipedes legs, which page would you look on?
- If you want to find out about animals with no legs, which pages would you look on?
- Look at page 10. Why do you think a starfish needs to grow a new leg?
- How do you think having no legs can help a snake?

EXPLORING LANGUAGE

Terminology
Title, cover, photographs, author, photographers

Vocabulary
Interest words: grow, centipede, insect, starfish, crab, claws
High-frequency words: lot, their, fast, goes, when
Positional words: on, off, in, out
Compound word: starfish

Print Conventions
Capital letter for sentence beginnings, periods, commas, exclamation mark